The Boy Who
BREAKFAST

By Eugene Bradley Coco
Illustrated by Ann Iosa

© 1992 McClanahan Book Company, Inc. All rights reserved.
Published by McClanahan Book Company, Inc.
23 West 26th Street, New York, NY 10010
Printed in Hong Kong

ISBN 1-56293-349-3

It was Saturday morning. The sun was shining, the birds were singing, and the sky was as blue as could be. Everyone on the farm was fast asleep except for Robby the Rooster who was sitting on the barn fence.

"It's almost time," said Robby as he looked at his alarm clock. Just then it started to ring, BRINGGGGG! BRINGGGGG!, and Robby cleared his throat, took a deep breath, and called out in as loud a voice as he could:

"Cock-A-Doodle-Doo! Cock-A-Doodle-Doo! It's time to wake up everyone! Cock-A-Doodle-Doo! Cock-A-Doodle-Doo!"

When Zach heard Robby's call, he opened his eyes, rolled out of bed, and quickly got dressed.

"I can't wait to play with all of my friends," he smiled, as he brushed his teeth, combed his hair, and raced downstairs.

"Good morning, Zach," called Zach's
mother from the kitchen.

"Good morning, Mom," said Zach.

"What would you like to eat for breakfast
today?" asked Zach's mother. "Pancakes?
Waffles? Eggs? Cereal? Toast? I can make
anything that you want."

"Have the pancakes," said Zach's sister Emma. "They taste so good. With sugar, and maple syrup, and strawberries, too."

"Try the cereal," said Zach's brother Jess. "It's so much fun when the apples and nuts crunch in your mouth."

"Sorry, but I don't have time to eat breakfast this morning," said Zach.

"But everyone has to eat breakfast," said Zach's mother. "It's the most important meal of the day."

"Not for me," said Zach. "I have other things to do."

Before Zach's mother could say another
word, Zach ran outside and into the meadow.
  Horace the Horse was standing under a tree
eating some hay when Zach ran over to him.

"Hi, Horace," said Zach.

"Hi, Zach," neighed Horace.

"Let's go for a ride in the hills," said Zach.
"We can play cowboy."

"I can't play with you right now," said
Horace. "I have to eat my breakfast. If I don't
eat breakfast, I won't be strong enough to carry
you on my back. By the way, what did you have
for breakfast this morning?"

"I didn't eat breakfast," said Zach.

"You must be hungry," said Horace. "Want some hay?"

"No thanks," said Zach. "Maybe we can play later."

Then Zach headed off to the barn looking for his friend Clara the Cow.

Clara was standing in her stall eating a bowl of grains and oats when Zach opened the barn door. It's almost milking time, thought Zach. That should be fun.

"Are you ready, Clara?" asked Zach as he brought over a stool and bucket.

"Not yet," said Clara. "I have to finish eating my breakfast. If I don't have something to eat, I won't be able to fill up that bucket with milk for you. Say, you're up early Zach. What did you have for breakfast this morning?"

"I didn't eat breakfast," said Zach.
"Why not?" asked Clara.
"I didn't have time," said Zach.

"Why, there's always time for breakfast,"
said Clara. "Would you like some grains and
oats? There's plenty left."

"No thanks," said Zach. "I have to be going anyway."

Zach ran over to the chicken coop to see his friend Cori the Chicken. It was egg-laying time, and one of Zach's favorite things to do was to watch Cori lay her eggs.

"Good morning, Cori," said Zach as he made his way into the chicken coop.

"Good morning, Zach," smiled Cori as she crunched on a kernel of corn.

"Have you laid any eggs yet?" asked Zach.
"No," said Cori. "I haven't eaten my
breakfast. If I don't eat breakfast, I can't lay any
eggs. Didn't you have breakfast this morning?"

"No," said Zach.
"Why not?" asked Cori.
"I don't need to," said Zach. "I'm not hungry."

Zach went outside. There was no one to play with. All of his friends were busy eating breakfast. Suddenly, he heard a rumbling in his

stomach. Then he heard a grumbling. Then he
heard a rumbling AND a grumbling. That could
mean only one thing. Zach ran home as fast as
he could.

"Is it too late to eat breakfast, Mom?" asked Zach.

"Not at all," smiled Zach's mother. "What would you like?"

"I'll have pancakes . . . and waffles . . . and eggs . . . and cereal . . . and toast."

When Zach finished eating, the rumbling
and grumbling in his stomach stopped. Horace
and Clara and Cori were waiting for him outside.
"How was breakfast?" they asked.
"It was DELICIOUS!" said Zach. "I can't
wait for lunch."